# DANCING WITH THE STAR

by Alex Harvey
illustrated by Stephen Reed

Ready-to-Read

Simon Spotlight/Nickelodeon
New York London Toronto Sydney New Delhi

Based on the TV series *SpongeBob SquarePants*™ created by Stephen Hillenburg
as seen on Nickelodeon™

SIMON SPOTLIGHT
An imprint of Simon & Schuster Children's Publishing Division
1230 Avenue of the Americas, New York, New York 10020

For information about special discounts for bulk purchases, please contact
Simon & Schuster Sales at 1-866-506-1949 or business@simonandschuster.com
Manufactured in the United States of America 1211 LAK
First Edition
2 4 6 8 10 9 7 5 3 1
ISBN 978-1-4424-3487-5 (pbk)
ISBN 978-1-4424-4162-0 (hc)

“Pearl, my girl, what are you watching?” Mr. Krabs asked. “You have not left the couch for two whole hours!”

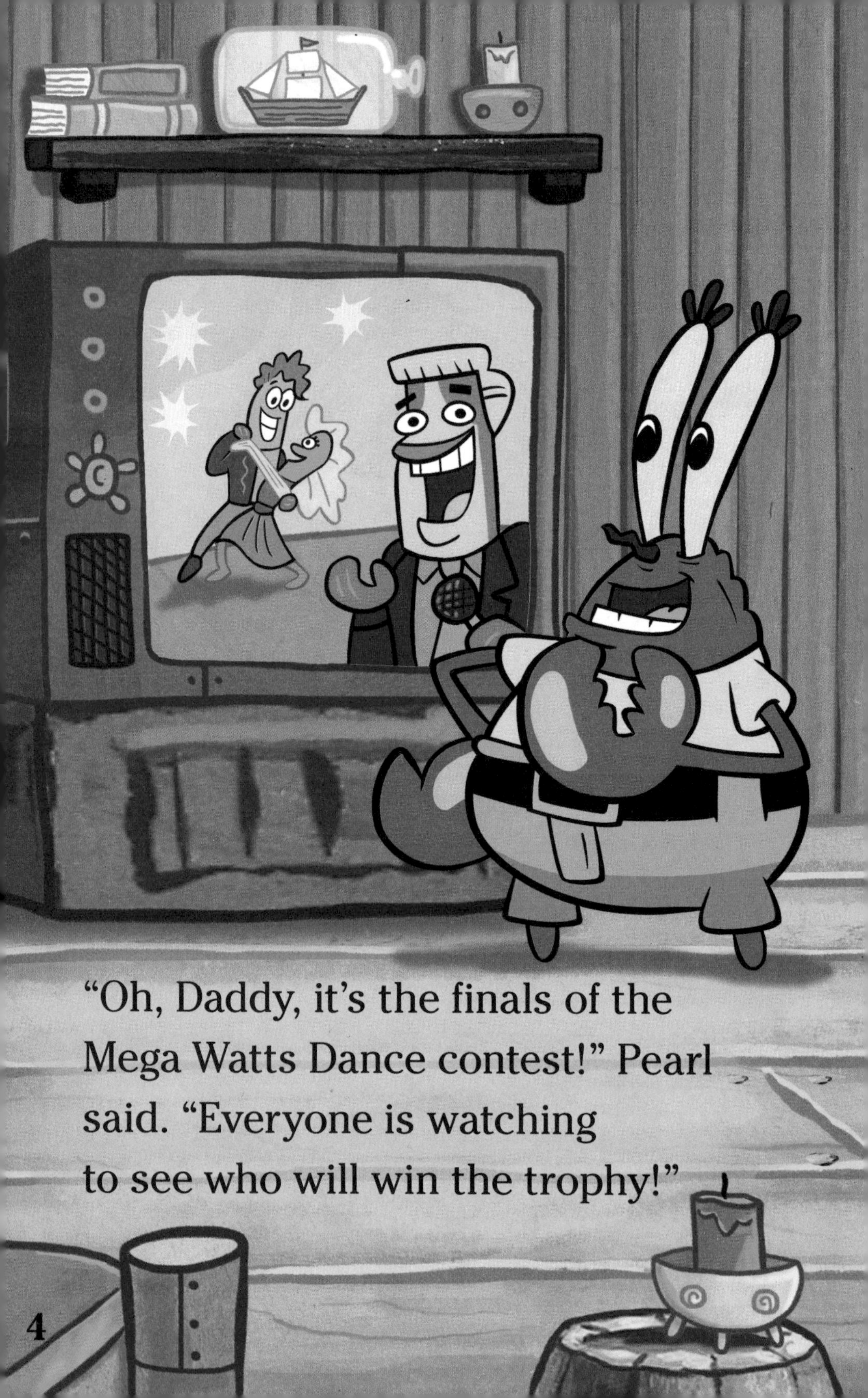

"Oh, Daddy, it's the finals of the Mega Watts Dance contest!" Pearl said. "Everyone is watching to see who will win the trophy!"

Mr. Krabs peered at the TV. "Why, that's Tom Sturgeon! He was my best buddy way back when. Who knew he would end up as the host of this show?"

"Daddy, I can't believe you know Tom Sturgeon!" Pearl squealed. "Do you think you can get him to visit? All my friends will think you are so coral!"

Mr. Krabs thought for a moment. "Why, that's a great idea, Pearl," he said. "Maybe he can even host a dance contest at the Krusty Krab. If people are as crazy about dancing as you say, we can make a little money here."

The next day Mr. Krabs told Squidward and SpongeBob, “We are going to have a dance contest at the Krusty Krab. My old friend Tom Sturgeon will be here to host it. And . . . we are going to have a lot of customers!”

"Can we be in the contest too?" SpongeBob asked.
"Well, as long as you make sure the customers are happy, I do not see why not," Mr. Krabs said.

"Oh, Squidward, isn't this exciting?
I am going to practice my best moves!"
SpongeBob said.
"Save yourself the trouble, SpongeBob,"
Squidward said. "I am going to win
this contest hands down. Oh, ha-ha,
I mean, feet down!"

SpongeBob and Squidward put up flyers all over Bikini Bottom. Soon everyone was talking about the dance contest.

Krusty Krab!
Dance Contest!
SHAKE YOUR FINS!
Dance Contest at the Krusty Krab!
SHOW OFF YOUR BEST MOVES!
CONTEST
Become a DANCING STAR!
DANCE! DANCE! DANCE!

Sandy was sure her Texas two-step would win her the trophy.

“I will wow everyone
with my cha-cha-cha,”
said Larry the Lobster.

SpongeBob found Patrick staring at a flyer. “Are you going to enter the contest?” SpongeBob asked.

“I am not sure, SpongeBob,” said Patrick. “I mean, I would like to.

DANCE CONTEST
AT THE KRUSTY KRAB

I have always dreamed of becoming a dancing star, but . . ."

Patrick looked so sad that SpongeBob decided to help him.

Krusty Krab Dance Off
Be there or be square (pants)

"I had no idea you loved to dance!" SpongeBob said. "I was going to enter, but I would rather help you win it!"

"Are you sure, SpongeBob?" Patrick asked.

“Of course,” said SpongeBob.
“You are my best buddy.
Now show me what you can do.”

At SpongeBob's house, SpongeBob turned on the music.
Patrick started to dance. Or rather he twisted and flopped on his belly and even stood on his head.

“Uh, Patrick, what are you doing?” SpongeBob asked.
“I am dancing!” Patrick said.

“I am not sure you can call that dancing,” said SpongeBob.
“But these are my best moves,” said Patrick.

“Hmm . . . I have an idea,”
SpongeBob said.

SpongeBob taught Patrick
a few other moves.

Soon Patrick was ready!

The Krusty Krab was filled with people on the day of the contest. "Greetings, everyone!" Tom said.

“Welcome to the Krusty Krab’s Love to Dance contest! Our judges today are Len Dory, Bruno Trout, and Pearl Krabs! Now let’s see who has the best moves in Bikini Bottom!”

Squidward called his dance
"Pure Elegance."
He leaped and stood on his toes.
He started to twirl around and
around and around.
Suddenly he was all tangled up!

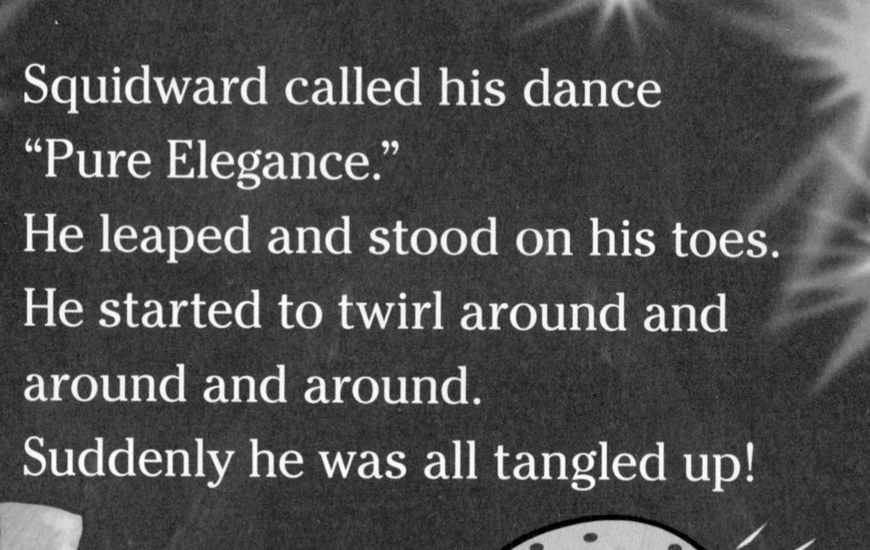

Everyone clapped along as Sandy
did the Texas two-step.
Mrs. Puff danced the Charleston.

Larry muttered "one-two-cha-cha-cha" as he danced.
Even Plankton did the jitterbug with his wife, Karen.

Finally it was Patrick's turn.
He was nervous until SpongeBob
gave him the thumbs-up sign.
Then the music started,
and Patrick was ready.

Patrick began to moonwalk,
then he did a backflip and landed
with a split! The crowd went wild!
Patrick danced smoothly across the
floor—

and in time to the music.

"Now, that's dancing!" Tom Sturgeon said. And the judges agreed.

“Look at that, Patrick. You are a dancing star!” said SpongeBob.